Vixen

by Penny Dolan and Katie Rewse

W

FRANKLIN WATTS

LONDON•SYDNEY

Vixen padded across the road.
An apple core lay by the litter bin
so she snatched it up with her sharp teeth
and ate it.

She trotted off along a path that ran between
the houses and through to the back gardens.
In one of those gardens was Vixen's special den.

Vixen ran along between tall weeds and gaps in fences.

Wait! What was that? Vixen sat still, scratching her ear and listening.

Suddenly, a dog charged across the lawn
towards her, barking fiercely.

Vixen jumped over the fence and
darted away. She was too quick for him.

Vixen trotted past flowerbeds and ponds

and garden sheds until she reached

a house with an overgrown garden.

An old man lived in the house last year

but he had gone away.

Was anyone there now?

At the far end of the garden,

under the rickety shed, was Vixen's old den.

She dug out earth and leaves until

she could squeeze into the den once more.

The following evening, Vixen poked her nose
out of the den. There were lights on
in the house. Vixen watched and waited
but nobody came down to the far end
of the garden. Her den still felt safe.

Vixen's mate, Fox, came to visit the garden too.
They greeted each other with wild screams
and barks and chased about in the moonlight.

Every night, Vixen dug up worms and beetles and ate roots from nearby vegetable patches. She stored mice in the ground to eat later.

Soon, Vixen stayed inside the den and had three tiny fox cubs.

They were covered in soft black fur

and nuzzled at her side.

Fox came and looked after Vixen

and the cubs, too.

In a while, the cubs' eyes opened.

Soon they were big enough to crawl out
of the den.

Vixen watched as the cubs tumbled about
on the grass. She saw them chase their tails
and play hide-and-seek among the plants.

Slowly, their fur turned fox red.

Vixen watched the house as well.
She saw people looking at
her playful cubs, but nobody came
to worry them at all.

However, one day, something worrying
did happen.

A delicious smell floated out of the house
and all the way up the garden.

The cubs stopped and sniffed and padded
towards the kitchen door.

They stared right in at all the food.

Some children were staring out at them, too.

"No!" warned Vixen. "Come away!
Foxes don't belong in houses!"

Quickly, she took her cubs back to the den.

Summer passed.

Vixen's cubs grew bigger and stronger.

One by one, they left the garden

and looked for dens of their own.

One cub went to live in a small wood,

and one padded off to the canal.

The youngest fox cub dug herself a new den

in a vegetable garden.

Vixen lay quietly near her den and listened to the children playing outside the house.

"This den was in a good place," she thought.

"Nobody bothered us after all. Perhaps I will have cubs in this garden again."

Then Vixen had a nap. Soon it would be time for her to set off on her own adventures once more.

Story order

Look at these 5 pictures and captions.
Put the pictures in the right order
to retell the story.

1

Vixen had three tiny cubs.

2

The cubs played in the garden.

3

Fox came to visit Vixen.

4

Vixen found her old den.

5

The cubs looked for their own homes.

Independent Reading

This series is designed to provide an opportunity for your child to read on their own. These notes are written for you to help your child choose a book and to read it independently.

In school, your child's teacher will often be using reading books which have been banded to support the process of learning to read. Use the book band colour your child is reading in school to help you make a good choice. *Vixen* is a good choice for children reading at Gold Band in their classroom to read independently.

The aim of independent reading is to read this book with ease, so that your child enjoys the story and relates it to their own experiences.

About the book

Vixen finds her old den under a shed. The shed is in the overgrown garden of a house that used to belong to an elderly man. She plans to have her cubs there. But the elderly man no longer lives in the house. Who is there now, and will Vixen's family be safe?

Before reading

Help your child to learn how to make good choices by asking: "Why did you choose this book? Why do you think you will enjoy it?" Look at the cover together and ask: "What do you think the story will be about?" Ask your child to read the title aloud. Ask whether they already know what a vixen is. Ask: "Do you think the story will be all about what Vixen does?" Remind your child that they can sound out the letters to make a word if they get stuck.

Decide together whether your child will read the story independently or read it aloud to you.

During reading

Remind your child of what they know and what they can do independently. If reading aloud, support your child if they hesitate or ask for help by telling the word. If reading to themselves, remind your child that they can come and ask for your help if stuck.

After reading

Support comprehension by asking your child to tell you about the story. Use the story order puzzle to encourage your child to retell the story in the right sequence, in their own words. The correct sequence can be found on the next page.

Help your child think about the messages in the book that go beyond the story and ask: "Why do you think Vixen is nervous about the new family in the house? Why does she tell her cubs off for going too near the house?"

Give your child a chance to respond to the story: "Have you ever seen a fox, or perhaps other wildlife, living near your home? How can you help wild animals if you see them living around humans?"

Extending learning

Help your child predict other possible outcomes of the story by asking: "If the new family in the house had not wanted Vixen and her cubs in their garden, what do you think might have happened? Where might she have gone to live?"

In the classroom, your child's teacher may be teaching different kinds of sentences. There are many examples in this book that you could look at with your child, including statements, commands, exclamations and questions. Find these together and point out how the end punctuation can help us decide what kind of sentence it is.

Franklin Watts
First published in Great Britain in 2020
by The Watts Publishing Group

Series Editors: Jackie Hamley and Melanie Palmer
Series Advisors: Dr Sue Bodman and Glen Franklin
Series Designers: Peter Scoulding and Cathryn Gilbert

A CIP catalogue record for this book is
available from the British Library.

ISBN 978 1 4451 7183 8 (hbk)
ISBN 978 1 4451 7184 5 (pbk)
ISBN 978 1 4451 7315 3 (library ebook)

Printed in China

Franklin Watts
An imprint of
Hachette Children's Group
Part of The Watts Publishing Group
Carmelite House
50 Victoria Embankment
London EC4Y 0DZ

An Hachette UK Company
www.hachette.co.uk

www.reading-champion.co.uk

Answer to Story order: 4, 3, 1, 2, 5